James Finlayson

Surnames & sirenames

The origin and history of certain family & historical names

James Finlayson

Surnames & sirenames
The origin and history of certain family & historical names

ISBN/EAN: 9783337271275

Printed in Europe, USA, Canada, Australia, Japan

Cover: Foto ©Raphael Reischuk / pixelio.de

More available books at **www.hansebooks.com**

SURNAMES & SIRENAMES.

THE

ORIGIN AND HISTORY

OF CERTAIN

FAMILY & HISTORICAL NAMES:

with

Remarks on the Ancient Right of the Crown to Sanction and Veto the Assumption of Names.

AND

AN HISTORICAL ACCOUNT OF THE NAMES

BUGGEY AND BUGG.

BY JAMES FINLAYSON.

"I, THE LORD, HAVE EVEN CALLED THEE BY THY NAME :
I HAVE SURNAMED THEE."   *Isaiah* xlv. 4.

"THERE ARE THREE CROWNS—THE CROWN OF THE LAW, THE CROWN OF THE PRIESTHOOD,
AND THE CROWN OF ROYALTY ; BUT THE CROWN OF A GOOD NAME is
SUPERIOR TO THEM ALL."   *The Talmud.*

"We'll keep our customs, what is Law itself,
............but old established custom?"—*Old Play.*

LONDON :

SIMPKIN, MARSHALL, AND CO.,

MANCHESTER: JOHN HEYWOOD, DEANSGATE.

TO

THE HON. ALEXANDER WILLIAM CRAWFORD,

LORD LINDSAY OF BALCARRES, F.S.A., G.S., &c., &c.,

THE FOLLOWING PAGES ARE INSCRIBED

IN

PROFOUND ADMIRATION OF THE RESEARCH AND LEARNING

HIS LORDSHIP

HAS SHOWN IN THE SUBJECT OF WHICH THEY TREAT AS WELL AS IN THE

HIGHER CLASSES OF

ARCHÆOLOGY AND GENEALOGY,

BY HIS LORDSHIP'S

MOST HUMBLE SERVANT,

J. F.

CONTENTS.

Part I.

CORRECTIONS.

———

Page 6.   Line 13.—For "Artrides"   read " Atrides."

,, 57.   ,,   17.— ,,   " bear"   ,,   " boar."

,, 57.   ,,   19.— ,,   " haris"   ,,   " heris."

,, 62.   ,,   36.— ,,   " Pemberton's" ,,   " Pembertons."

Part II.

CONTENTS.

Part I.

Part II.

INTRODUCTION.

What should be in that Cæsar?
Why should that name be sounded more than yours?
Write them together, yours is as fair a name;
Sound them, it doth become the mouth as well;
Weigh them, it is as heavy; conjure with them,
Brutus will start a spirit as soon as Cæsar.

JULIUS CÆSAR, A. I., S. II.

SURNAMES at the present day do not seem to give the same satisfaction to those who bear them as in times past, hence there has arisen a most extraordinary anxiety to exchange those—the worth of which their owners are not aware of—for names that seem to them to be more euphonious, or of greater historic renown.

The most notable instance is that of the exchange of Bugg for Howard—a good exchange; but Mr. Bugg could not have been aware of the origin of his name, or he might have exchanged it for one out of many to which he had an undoubted right, without infringing, as he clearly has done, upon the property of a noble house: for a man's name is a man's property, just as much as houses and lands are property.

This proprietorship is not so well known or understood as it ought to be; and the honourable member for Sheffield fell into a prevalent, but erroneous opinion on the subject, when he stated from his place in Parliament, that "any man has a right to take any name he pleases, upon any occasion he pleases, and for any reason he pleases." This is not the case; and from time immemorial the Crown has been called upon either to sanction or veto the assumption of surnames. This right the Crown still possesses.

Before entering more fully upon this question of the right of the Crown, I propose discussing the general history of sire-names and surnames, their antiquity, use, and abuse; concluding with a list of popular English names, their origin and meaning.

—⤙⤚✦⟨⟩✦⤙⤚—

PART I.

—◦◦)※(◦◦—

CHAPTER I.

It has been said in the House of Commons that " it was only quite lately that Surnames as Surnames had been had at all." Surnames as surnames proper were in existence even long before Jacob was surnamed Israel, as the following references will prove. It is a fact well known to all Egyptologists, that the ancient Kings of Egypt had more than one or two surnames besides their sire-names, (Eratosthenes). On the surnames of the ancient Egyptians of all classes, Sir William Gardner thus speaks:—" The aversion to change as to all things in Egypt extended even to names, which seldom varied in the same family." Hence we have the *sire* and surnames with their prænomen of most of the kings, many of whom might vie with a Spanish prince of the present day in the multiplicity of their names. Mons. A. Bockh deciphered a contract of sale effected in Egypt 104 years before our era, the names of the contracting parties, being not only described in the deeds by their proper names, but by a detailed description of their physical peculiarities. (Salverte, 67.)

During the Homeric age, local names as surnames
and patronymics were not uncommon.

Homer Melesigenes himself, the most ancient author
of the heathen world, almost three thousand years
ago, received a local surname from his mother, owing
to his birth occurring on the banks of the river Meles,
through her incontinency when single. His universal
name was given him, as is well known by the
Cumæans, from his blindness.

In the opening of the " Iliad" we are told that a
priest of " Chrysa's shores," named " Chryses," had a
daughter called " Chryseis," the captive concubine of
Agamemnon *Atrides*.

In another case we have a local surname and a
patronymic in the person of
"The *young Astyanax*, the hope of Troy."
"To this loved infant Hector gave the name
Scamandrius, from Scamander's honor'd stream."

He receives the first name from the people.
" Astyanax, the Trojans called the boy,
From his great father, the defence of Troy."
And then again, the
" Fair Simoisius, whom his mother bore,
Amid the flocks, on silver Simois' shore;
*   *   *   *   *
And thence from Simois nam'd the lovely boy."
The name Ajax was evidently a patronymic or
family name.
"   *   *   *   Oileus came;
Him *Ajax* honor'd with a *brother's name*,
Though born of lawless love, from home expell'd."

We also read of "Ajax the less, and Ajax Telamon."
And again, " the Ajaces next succeed."

In China at the present day, the family name is
always placed first, and is followed by a numerous
variety of surnames of great antiquity, which is the
ancient mode of using names. The Kings of Egypt
were surnamed Pharaoh, so, the regal successors of

Alexander Mægas, or the Great, acted in accordance with the custom of the country in changing such proper names as Ptolemy, Seleucus, and Antiochus, into a hereditary title and a surname, instance Ptolemy Sotor, Ptolemy Philadelpheus, Ptolemy Euergetes, Ptolemy Philopator, Ptolemy Epiphanes, Ptolemy Philometor, Ptolemy Neüs Dionysus. The Hebrews, *Hebrew Sirenames their antiquity.* during the period of their kings, used the name of their father, with the name of their tribe, in addition to Ben., *i.e.,* son, as Melchi Ben Addi, Addi Ben Cosam.

Surnames were introduced at a very early period among the Israelites ; their practice, as appears from the Scriptures, seems to have been that of adding the name of the father to that of the son, as Caleb the son of Jephunneh, and Joshua the son of Nun, being equivalent to Jephunnehson and Nunson. Again, among the apostles, we find several who are known to us by their surnames, " Lebbæus, whose surname was Thaddæus" according to St. Matthew ; St. Mark, mentions him, by his surname only ; we read in the same Gospel of Simon the Canaanite, but in Luke the same person is named Simon Zelotes. Our Saviour surnamed Simon, *Peter*, but when he *Scriptural Instance of Surname and Sirename.* appeared to his disciples at the great draught of fishes, and after he had dined with them, " Jesus saith to Simon Peter, Simon, *son* of Jonas."—John xxi. Now the Hebrew equivalent for son is *Bar*, which we shall find explains itself in Matthew, 16 c., 17 v., " Jesus answered and said unto him," (Simon Peter), " Blessed art thou, Simon *Bar-jona*." in this name we find the hyphen introduced to note greater distinction, we also find a remarkable clearness of distinguishing father and son in the case of the blind beggar of Jericho, who is called "blind *Bartimæus*, the son of Timæus," here the person is only known to us by his sire-name, his name of circumcision is not given, but "blind" is substituted, this name probably some gentlemen would term a nickname. "And James, the son of Zebedee, and John the brother of James ; he (Jesus) surnamed them *Boanerges*, which is, the sons of Thunder." St. Paul tells us of John, whose surname was *Mark*, and of Judas surnamed *Bar-sabas*," and of "a false prophet, a Jew, whose (sire) name was *Bar-jesus*," "and Simeon that was called Niger," or Simon Black ; Joses was surnamed *Barnabas* ; Judas *Bar-sabas*, and his brother "Joseph *Bar-sabas*, who was surnamed *Justus*," and of Zacharias, son of *Bar-achias*. Judas *Iscariot* derived his surname from his estate ; according to the Rabbins, Moses had seven other names, Moses being the name given at circumcision.

Instances of Sirenames and Surnames in one and the same person.

It cannot be implied in speaking historically that because we are unacquainted with the prænomens of the great men of Britain some 1800 years ago, that they had nothing of the sort. We must not assert that the ancient Britons had only one name during their lifetime for all purposes, private and public. I am aware that the most learned men have stated such to be the case, yet withal, I firmly believe, that every person of any position, in the most barbarous ages, has had at least two names, the first, that which the person would be known by among his own family (a home name, in fact) the pro-totype of our Christian name ; but when of age and embarked in the turmoils of life, another name would be given, either from a personal defect, some characteristic trait, or from circumstances by which the bearer would be known among his own people ; again, it often happened that a name given by a neighbouring people became the first or the most honoured surname with the bearer.

On the existence of British Surnames.

Can we for a moment imagine that the Celtic or

ancient British people, who gave such beautiful, descriptive and expressive compound names to the rivers, mountains, hills, and towns, in these islands. should themselves be without an individual surname? The people who so accurately described the physical features of certain localities with the following prefixes:—Col, Fal, Pen, Tor or Dor, Tre, Man, Men, or Mon, Caer, Llud, Pol, &c., were not the stultards they are erroneously believed to be. Cæsar in his G. W. b. v. c. 10, dispels this fallacy, in his remarks on surnames, which he speaks of very pointedly, he says, "those who dwelt in the maritime part of Britain, had passed over out of Belgium, who almost all were called by the names of the cities or states, from which they came." So far, this proves that local names had then become personal names, some score years before the coming of Christ. And again, it was usual among the ancient Britons, or before Cæsar's flying visit to these shores, for the son to assume the prefix of the father's surname, thus identifying the bearer with his family and certain qualities which he possessed. The earliest instance known in our history of such a name is that of Imanuentius or Man-uentius, King of the Trinobantes (Essex), who was murdered by Cassibellaunus, the chief of Hertford. *Avarwy* Man-dubratius the son of Man-uentius fled to Gaul and implored Cæsar's protection before his invasion. This practice, continued until the latter part of the sixth century, (A.D. 577), as shown by M. Villemarque in the poems of the Bards of Breton," edited by him, one of which runs thus:—" I lament for thee *Cynd*-helan, fair son of *Cynd*-rouyn, for a man who is no better than a maiden is not fitting to wear a beard about the nostril."

Antiquity of local names as Surnames in Britain.

Ancient British Sirenames.

Camden says—" the like was used among our

ancestors the English, as Ceon-red, Ceolwalding, Ceold-
wald Cutting, Cuth Cuthwinning, that is Ceonred,
sonne of Ceolwald Ceolwald, sonne of Cuth Cuth,
sonne of Cuthwin, &c." (Remaines, 106.)

Ancient British Surnames. The above are names of descent. I will cite now
the names of the brothers Caractacus and Togodumnus,
both British circumstantial surnames, and which are
extremely expressive. The first signifies " the beloved chieftain of the hill fortresses," the second, " the
leader of the people of the valleys."

Shakes-peare's Definition of a Surname. The Britons, as a rule, gave surnames which
Shakespeare, in his play of Richard II., characterises
as " O, how that name befits my composition !"
Caractacus had also the surname " Caradoc," Car or
Caer, a fort, and dog or dug, a commander, (latinized duc,
English duke). Probably the hill fortresses under his
command would be those of Car-narvon, Car-marthen,
Cardiff, Car-leon, and Car-peilly, at which places the
Britons erected fortresses. We may be sure that Caractacus was not so named until after he had adopted a system of offensive warfare against the Romans, and which
certainly originated his name. Mr. Wright in men-
tioning this illustrious chief in his admirable work on
the Celt, Roman and Saxon, says, "that he chose a
strong position on a lofty hill on the river Ony, near the
confluence Chun and the Tame, in the south-western
part of Shropshire, still called Caer-Caradoc, (and)
has been supposed to be the scene of the final defeat
of Caractacus." It may here be asked, by what name
was this famous British hero previously known to his
family and to his tribe,—are we to suppose that he
had none ?

There are other names of ancient Britons equally
full of meaning, as Mynydd-dog, the mountain-com-
mander ; Llywarch, the daring adventurer, and
Avarwy or Androgeus, surnamed *Du-bradwr*, Mandu-
brad, the Black Traitor.

The ancient Britons were divided into families, tribes, and states, which division gave them a correct knowledge of their pedigrees and relationship. Kindred was acknowledged to the *sixth degree ;* we rarely acknowledge the fourth cousin-german, yet the laws of Hoel say, "that there is not an appropriate name for relationship beyond that degree ;" yet it is generally understood that kindred extended to the *ninth* degree ; and that all who desired to maintain the privileges of natives were obliged to establish, at least, this degree of kindred ; since those who failed were reduced to the condition of aliens, hence the absolute necessity of preserving some family name which would identify the owner with his father and his tribe.

Pedigrees of the Britons and their necessity of preserving a Family Name.

" When we observe attentively the vast importance attached to the exact knowledge of an individual's degree of consanguinity to other members of the same tribe; when we consider the care and attention which parents would naturally bestow in teaching accurately to their children the different degrees of relationship which the various members of a family bore to each other, a knowledge which under particular circumstances might be of vast beneficial importance to possess, and of great detriment, inconvenience, and loss to be ignorant of ; we may then account, perhaps wholly, for the peculiar hereditary attention which our Cambrian brother subjects pay to the transmission of their family names and pedigrees ; a degree of attention which appears so strikingly remarkable, perhaps we may say so strikingly ridiculous, to one of that ' mixed multitude, ' the Englishers,' or ' Sassenach,' whose whole genealogical knowledge generally

Native Welsh Pedigrees.

Compared with English Genealogy

* According to the poem, the British town Treun, had been destroyed, and the question was, should Cynd-helan restore it, and join a confederacy of the British tribes.—*Quarterly Rev.* vol. 91, p. 282.

B

consists in merely knowing that his 'father was a Yorkshireman,' or 'that his family came out of Worcestershire,' and that he has a great many relations somewhere, only he does not know where to look for them."

The Messrs Burke in their Encyclopædia of Armory of the British Empire thus testify to the transmission of Welsh pedigrees ; they say—"their chroniclers and bards flourished from the remotest times as genealogists and heralds, and the collections and pedigrees of those patriarchal poets are still regarded as the foundation of Cambrian family history."

The recent finding of gold chains in Sussex of the ancient Celtic kings brings to mind an event mentioned in history which bears upon the subject of circumstantial names. At Amiens, Manlius, in a single combat took a golden chain from a Senonian Gaul, which obtained him the surname of Torquatus. (Florus, B. 1, C. 13.) Cæsar, in his (G. W. b. 1. c. 16,) names a particular friend of his Divitiacus (the) Æduan, who was both a Druid, and a person of the first consequence in the state. Salverte says that instances of inscriptions have been interpreted by Passeri, which clearly prove that the Etrurians had names, prænomina, and surnames, a great number of which are reproduced in Roman names; among which people surnames began early to be used as hereditary distinctions ; being derived, as names were anciently, from some qualification of the bearer, or event in his history, as in that of Torquatus ; others again say that they first introduced the use of hereditary names on the occasion of their league with the Sabines ; for the confirmation of which it was agreed, that the Romans should prefix Sabine names, and

[margin note:] Etrurian Surname.

[margin note:] Roman Surname.

the Sabines, Roman names to theirs. At a much The nature of Roman names. later period the Romans generally had three names. The first, called *prænomen*, answered to our Christian name, and was intended to distinguish the individuals of the same family; the second, called *nomen*, corresponded to the word *clan* in Scotland, and was given to all those who were sprang from the same stock; the third, called *cognomen*, expressed the particular branch of the tribe or clan from which any individual was sprang, the agnomen, or another surname, taken from some remarkable action. The names of the Scipios afford a good illustration of the manner of conferring names among the Romans. They sprang from the illustrious family of the Cornelii, of which the Scipios, the Lentuli, &c., were branches. Both family names were retained by each male member of the family, and a first name was conferred to distinguish the individual. Thus, one brother was termed Publius Cornelius Scipio, the Explanation of Roman Collective names. other Lucius Cornelius Scipio; and in the case of the conqueror of Carthage, the agnomen Africanus was conferred as a memorial of his military prowess. With regard to the names of the first person here named—*Publius* corresponded to our names John, Robert, William, &c.; *Cornelius* was the name of the *clan* or tribe, as Campbell was formerly the name of all the Duke of Argyle's tenants, and Douglas the name of the retainers of the Duke of Hamilton's progenitors. *Scipio* being added, conveyed this information, that Publius, who was of the tribe of Cornelii, was of the family of the Scipios, one of the branches or families into which that tribe was divided. In Rome, family names were hereditary sirenames, but surnames were individual, and almost all of them either given or " sanctioned by the public voice." Respecting the names of the British chiefs, there is ample evidence to prove that the sons of such worthies were instructed by command of Agricola in the language and knowledge of their conquerors. Palgrave tells us, that " the Britons learnt to speak the Latin language, & adopted Latin names." "The manners of the Romans also gradually took root among them."

Early instance of the assumption of names by Imperial authority in Britain. A notable instance of the adoption of a prænomen and nomen is to be found in the person of the British prince Cogidubnus, chief of the Regni in Sussex, who, according to Tacitus, assumed the name of the Emperor Tiberius Claudius, in addition to his own. Cogidubnus assumed the above names with the Emperor's sanction, and which I believe is the earliest instance of a Briton adopting the name of another.

A Roman British soldier with two names. Horsley gives an instance of a surname inscribed on a fragment of a votive tablet found at Ebchester, in Durham, dedicated to the Goddess Minerva by Julius *Gueneius*, a Briton, who is styled—A Ctvarivs Cohortis. IIII. BR.*; and another instance, which Mr. Wright thus speaks of :—" The pedestal of a statue, which probably represented a figure of Britannia, was dug up at York in the middle of last century, with the inscription—

A free Roman Briton with two names.

To Sacred
Britain
Publius Nicomedes
of our two emperors
the freedman.

which clearly proves that the dedicator had not only two names, but was also a free Briton.

Florus, in speaking of the Celts, and having occasion to speak of Vercingetorix, says he was "terrible both in person, arms, and spirit, *his very name,*

---

* Wright's Celt, &c., p. 225.

too, being framed, as it were, to excite terror." (B. iii., c. 10.) Indeed! names were so freely given among the Britons, as surnames, that the man who maimed himself, by cutting off his thumb, for fear of going to the wars, was called ever afterward Murco—coward, (A. Marcell, B. xv., c. 12), and which, doubtless, would be coupled with his former names. *(A British surname of contempt.)*

We read in the recorded poetry of the ancient bards of Britain the account of the celebrated battles of *Gwallog Galcagus,* the chief of the Scots, who so eminently signalized himself in opposing the onward march of the Roman legions into the Highlands, "That he, and *Dunawd ab Pabo,* and *Cynfelyn Drwsgwl,* were the three pillars of battle of the Isle of Britain" (A.D. 280). We also read of the following Welsh chiefs possessed of sire and surnames:—Cynedda Gwladig, Caswallawn Llawhir, Maelgwn Gwynedd, Rhun ab Maelgwn, Cadwaladr Bendiged,* Rhiwallawn Walltbenhadlen, Cadwallawn ab Cadsan, Gafran ab Aeddan, Prince of the Picts, A.D. 550; Gwenddolan ab Ceidraw, King of the Picts, A.D. 554; and Donal Brech, a Gælic chieftain living in the Lowlands of Scotland, in the year 637. *(Britons of the 3rd and 4th centuries with sire and surnames.)*

And of the Pictish kings Angus *Mac Fergus,* A.D. 730, and his son, Constantine *Mac Fergus,* A.D. 789, and Kenneth Mac Alpine, A.D. 836. *(Ancient Scottish sirenames.)*

The proud British chief, Gwrthrigorn, surnamed Vortigern, was the first prince who held regal command in the field against the Picts and Scots after the Romans left Britain. Again, we read of *Ambrosius Aurelianus,* who first commanded the Britons against the Saxons, and of his son (Uter), surnamed by Merlin, Pendragon, who was also named Aurelius Uterius. King Arthur, who is scarcely known by any other name,—

---

* Bendiged is from *Bendigedig,* which means *blessed.* It changes into Fendiged according to the Welsh grammatical rule of mutations, that is, after prepositions and in the vocative case.

bore that of *Llywiadwr*, or Supreme Governor, by which alone he is described in the indisputably genuine poems of the sixth century. (Quar. Review, vol. 91, p. 299.)

Instances of ancient hereditary patronymics among the Jutes and the Angles.

There was another people much more barbarous than the Britons who had even hereditary *sire*names. Eric, the son of Hengist the Jute, and the ancestor of the Kings of Kent, was surnamed Æsc. His sons bore the patronymic *Æscingas*, or sons of Æsc. The same ancient mode of expressing descent was in being among the Kings of East Anglia, who were Angles. The sons of King Uffa bore the patronymic *Uffingas*. Moreover, even centuries later we find the sirename or patronymic in general use among the nobles or thanes. Thus, in a genealogy of the West Saxon Kings among the Cotton MSS., we read of Eadgar Eadmund*ing*, Eadmund Eadward-*ing*, Eadweard Aelfred-*ing*, Aelfred Awolf-*ing*.

Anglo-Saxon patronymics.

Brito-Saxon sirenames.

Nearly two hundred years later, we read that *Cyne*-wolf, King of the West Saxons, was murdered at Merton by his son, the Atheling *Cyne*-ard. Why, the most important designation in our language, that of king, is derived from that very people whom some individuals believe knew nothing of sirenames or surnames. It is derived from the Celtic word *cen* or *cean*, chief or head. The Anglo-Saxons would appear to have altered the word to Cynge, founder of a family —Kin—,*ing* being an Anglo-Saxon patronymic for son, as shown above.

The youngest son of Roderick the Great (who was King of Wales in the year 842), was surnamed *Tudwal Gloff;* and Prince Iorweth *Drwyndwn* of Powis. Malcolm *Ceanmoir*, in the year 1061, more than five years before the Norman conquest, summoned a general council of his Peers at Forfar, in order to settle the question of landed proprietors bearing surnames, which he wished to be territorial. Antiquity of Scottish and French local names compared. Indeed, about the year 800, in the reign of Kenneth II., the great men had begun to call *their names by their own lands*, as Shakespeare proves when he speaks of Macbeth as Cawdor and Glamis. Du Chesne observes that surnames were unknown in France before the year 987, when the lords began to assume the names of their demesnes.

M. Salverte, in speaking of the names of the Caledonians, says:—"The adoption of surnames soon became an absolute necessity, and accordingly we find Antiquity of Caledonian sirenames. that the Caledonians always joined their father's name to their own; Oscar, son of Ossian; Oscar, of Caruth; Dermid, son of Duthmo; Dermid, son of Diaran." He further remarks:—"The Caledonians were not less careful than the Arabs in the matter of their genealogies, and endeavoured to remedy, by uninterrupted Their genealogies and their nature. tradition, any confusion which might otherwise have arisen from the want of hereditary surnames. Pride of birth was not their only guarantee for the correctness of the tradition; there were two very powerful sentiments which combined to preserve it in its purity—the one affection, the other resentment. As these feelings were uninterruptedly transmitted from father to son, they served to remind people (with perfect accuracy of detail) of the various events which had led either to a firm alliance or to deadly enmity between two tribes. Such was the influence of their recollections, that two warrior chiefs who chanced to meet in battle would conceal their names, lest they should be suggestive of some common tie of kin or friendship, which might furnish an excuse for avoiding the encounter. A still more honourable fear dictated a rule, that no stranger who claimed hospitality should be asked his name before the expiration of three whole days, under pain of the most severe punishment the law could inflict.

During that time, all hereditary hatred that a name might rekindle had to lie dormant;—during that time a generous hospitality had to take the place of a thirst for revenge."

Again, among the Scots, the name of a village or town often gave the family name of the Lord of the Manor. Shakespeare most beautifully proves this when we hear Macbeth's self-accusations, as he reproaches himself by the titles of the lands of which he is thane, and exclaims, in the anguish of his remorse:—

> *Glamis* hath murther'd sleep: and therefore *Cawdor*
> Shall sleep no more, Macbeth shall sleep no more!
>
> Act ii., s. 2.

CHAPTER II.

In the course of the debate in the House of Commons, on the subject of names, Mr. Roebuck Mr. Roebuck's argument on Mr. Falconer's proposition considered. said "he would read a few sentences from a book of Mr. Falconer's, who was now a judge in Wales, which *really contained all the law upon the subject.*" The following is the passage referred to :—"That in the year 1735, when the question of the manner in which surnames could be changed was before the House of Lords, NO NOTICE *was taken of any supposed privilege of the Crown to grant licenses on such occasions"* There is some ambi- guity in this passage. What is the intended meaning of *no notice was taken?* If usage and custom become law, that law is still vested in the crown to sanction all assumptions of names to make them legal. Here Antiquity of the Crown and the Peers legalising a name of assumption is a case in point, which was brought before King Henry II. and his Peers in Parliament, when the application for the assumption of a surname (and that surname a local name) was granted and confirmed to the applicant and his heirs, and he was summoned thereto by that name. This statement may be verified on referring to the worthy Roger Dodsworth's MSS. in the Bodleian Library, Oxford. (Ex præfato Regist. de Cokersand. fo. 72. B.) A copy of this charter may also be found in Dodsworth's Monasticon, Dugdale's edition, Vol. 6, p. 909, entitled " Gilbertus Will. qui quidem Willielmus fecit se vocari Willielmum de Lancaster, et fecit se vocari coram rege in parlia- mento Willielmum de Lancaster, baronem de Ken- dale :" that is, Gilbert William, which said William

c

caused himself to be called William de Lancaster, and caused himself to be called in presence of the king in parliament, William de Lancaster, baron de Kendale.

Henry II. previously sanctions the assumption, but allows the same to be confirmed by the Peers. Now, from the known jealousy of Henry for his prerogative, De Lancaster must first have had permission granted him to bring his request before the Chamber. King Henry II. was not the sovereign that would sit and hearken to so much assumption from a subject, and that subject an officer of his court (sheriff of Lancaster), and the son of a justice of the King's Bench, without having sanctioned the preliminary steps.

I consider that the approval and confirmation by the House of Peers, over 700 years ago, is exactly in keeping with the "privilege of the crown to grant licenses" at the present day. Now, were the case just named not sufficient to prove the right of the crown Kings of England commanding certain nobles to assume surnames. to sanction assumptions, others, of a different phase, and, more imperative, can be adduced in a change of names by Royal command, which occurred during the reigns of Henry I., Edward I., and Henry VIII. For, it must hold good that, if the crown cannot sanction and legalise the assumption of a surname, so likewise it cannot command a subject to take upon him a particular name.

Assumption of the surname of Moubray "by the special command" of King Henry I. The first instance occurred in the year 1106. Nigel de Albini who, (according to the register of Furness Abbey, was bow-bearer to Rufus and Henry I.), at the battle of Trenchbray dismounted Robert, Duke of Normandy, and brought him prisoner to the king. Henry gave the lands of the attainted Robert Moubray, Earl of Northumberland, "in Normandy and England, to Nigel, as a reward for his great services and bravery:" and "by the special command of King Henry" he and his posterity were commanded to "assume the surname of Moubray" (Dugdale's Bar. vol. 1, p. 122);

which they accordingly did, and retained the same as long as the issue male continued, which determined in John Moubray, Duke of Norfolk, in the time of King Edward IV., whose heirs were married into the families of Howard and Barkley. Nigel de Albini was a Moubray maternally.

The second case of assumption by command occurred in the reign of King Edward I. who, disliking the iteration of Fitz in the name of a famous noble, Lord John Fitz Robert (whose ancestors had continued their sires' Christian names as surnames), to abandon that practice, and to bear the local name of the capital seat of his barony, (Clavering,) which command Lord John Fitz Robert complied with and became John de Clavering.

Assumption of a surname by command of Edward I.

The third case is that of the great-great-grandfather of the Protector, Richard Williams, a gentleman of good family in Wales, changed his name to Cromwell, in compliance with a wish (which there can be little doubt was equal to a command) of Henry VIII., taking that particular name in honour of his relative, Thomas Cromwell, Earl of Essex, then a favourite minister of that king, and whose sister Williams had married. (Dugdale's Bar. vol. 2, p. 374.

The following facts will prove the legality of this assumption by request. This Richard Cromwell on May day, 1540, at a great jousting at Westminster, which had been proclaimed in France, Spain, Scotland, and Flanders, was appointed one of the six challengers against all comers. On the second of May he was knighted by the King. On the third he did tourney with the other challengers against forty-nine. Stowe only notes the " overthrow of Master Palmer and his horse in the field," by Sir Richard ; and on the fifth of May the challengers fought on foot against fifty single handed, and again Sir Richard only is named by

Stowe as having done a feat of arms in overthrowing — Culpeper, Esq. It is a well known fact that the

The same sanctioned by the Court of Chivalry.

stringent laws enforced by the Court of Chivalry, or the Earl Marshal's Court, on the occasion of Jousts and Tournaments, debarred any person from entering the lists who had dared to take upon himself the surname of another illegally. Not only this, but no Knight of France, Scotland, or Spain, would demean himself by raising a lance with a man who bore not his lawful name and arms. From these instances of fact, I conclude it is proved that this usage was established and recognized by the King in the year 1106. and by the King and his Peers in the year 1160. Consequently, from the three cases cited, the Crown and Parliament have a prescriptive right to sanction all assumptive surnames before they can be considered perfectly legal. This was the law in 1160, the same law was held as binding in 1290, and it ought to be so held in 1863.

Payment of Fees.

There is this fact respecting the assumptions to be borne in mind, that neither Nigel de Moubray, William de Lancaster, John de Clavering, nor Sir Richard Cromwell paid a single mark for their assumption of said names that we know of ; yet, were nothing paid in any case into the exchequer, it would not affect or militate against the legality of the affair.

The Crown Vetoes the Assumption of a certain Surname.

Then again, on the other side, we have notable instances of the crown vetoing the assumption of sire or surnames in the following families. The original names of the Dukes of Beaufort, if the family were allowed to bear it, is Plantagenet. But, as the present Duke of Beaufort descends from the Plantagenets by a double bastardy, he has no right to any other name than that of Somerset. Sir Charles Somerset,

And Sanctions it in others.

natural son of Beaufort, Duke of Somerset, to which Beaufort's ancestor, a natural son of John of Gaunt, the name of Beaufort had been given. Yet another

base-born Plantagenet was permitted to bear that
royal name, the Viscount De L'Isle. The same rule
of vetoing also applies to the Dukes of Richmond, of
Grafton, and of St. Alban's, and did do to Monmouth ; they were not permitted by their father,
Charles II., to assume his name of Stuart, but had the
surnames of Lennox, Fitzroy, and Beauclerk. And
I may also cite the issue of George IV. And even
the senseless Caligula issued an order that the descendants of Pompey should be restrained from assuming
the surname of Magnus.

An Act of Parliament (10 Henry 7th, c. 20) was
passed interdicting and abolishing the Irish names or
words Crom-a-boo, Butler-a-Boo, &c.

By an act of the Scottish Privy Council, dated
3rd April, 1603, the name of Mac Gregor was
expressly abolished, and those who had hitherto
borne it were commanded to change it for other
surnames, the pain of death being denounced against
those who should call themselves Gregor or Mac
Gregor, the names of their fathers. By a sub-
sequent Act of Council, 24th June, 1613, death
was denounced against any person of the clan
called Mac Gregor. Again, by an Act of Parliament,
1617, chap. 26, these laws were continued, and extended to the rising generation, inasmuch as great
numbers of the children of those against whom the
acts of the Privy Council had been directed, were
stated to be then approaching to maturity, who, if
permitted to resume the name of their parents, would
render the clan as strong as it was before. But, upon the
Restoration, King Charles, in the first Scottish Parliament of his reign (statute 1661, chap. 195,) an-
nulled the various Acts against the clan Mac Gregor,
and restored them to the full use of their name.

The Surname of the Clan Mac Gregor proscribed.

We even find an ancient King of Egypt compelling
a tributary King of Judah to assume another name.

Instance of a Tributary King of Judah assuming a name by command of a King of Egypt. In the 2nd Book of Kings, 23c. 34v. we are told that "Pharaoh Nechoh, King of Egypt, made Eliakim, the son of Josiah, king in the room of Josiah his father, *and turned his name to Jeho*-iakim, and *took Jeho*-ahaz *away*," which was the name of his grandfather. Now it is very certain that this name was a modified sire-name, because we find that when "*Jeho*-iakim slept with his fathers, *Jeho*-iachin his son reigned in his stead." II. Kings, 24 c. 6 v.

The idea is erroneous "*that a man may assume what surname and as many surnames as he pleases*," by giving it publicity through the press, the very means to be adopted, as here held forth to affect that change, is a confession of wrong, provided, that the name coveted be not one of consanguinity. Again, a name cannot be legally used "by deed enrolled in Chancery," such contrivance was only put into practice, by two brothers of the name of Adams, in October, 1851.

Shakespeare's Opinion on the Illegal Assumption of Surnames. The illegal assumption of surnames was not tolerated during the days of Shakespeare, he most emphatically condemns it in his play "Taming of the Shrew."

> PETRUCIO.—"Why, how now gentleman! why, this is flat knavery, to take upon him another man's name."—Act. 5. Sc. 1.

It may be said that "Shakespeare alludes to the assumption of a man's name for the nonce," even so, the immortal bard however expresses his abhorrence of such knavery in other plays. Camden quotes a common saying of his time ridiculing such covetousness; he writes "that a gentlewoman, Docter Andreas the great civilian's wife said; '*If fair names were saleable, they would be well bought.*' "—Rem. p. 153.

Marie-Antoine Conti, of Majoraggio, in Milan, changed his name to Marcus Antonius *Majoraggius*, only adopting the name of his native town with a latin termination; such an uproar was made about it that he was positively driven to write a treatise to prove that he had a right to change his name without incurring any blame.

It is a most remarkable fact that the men who first petitioned the Secretary of State for a change of name, were returned convicts desirous of assuming other names and a new course of life.

In Spain it is necessary to procure a license from the Sovereign to change a name.

In France an express law relative to the false assumption of surnames and changes of names of the II. Germinal of the year XI., was enacted, it runs thus:—

> ART. IV.—Every person who has any reason for changing his name, shall address a demand to Government stating his motives.
>
> ART. V.—The Government shall decide in the form prescribed by the regulations of public administrations.

According to the law of 1858, all cases are now carried to the court of the Procureur Impérial.

The Prussian provincial law (Landrecht), part ii., title xx., s. 14, 406, enacts, "Whoever, even without illegal intention, assumes a family name, or arms, without right, shall be forbidden the assumption under pain of an arbitrary, but express fine; and this punishment, in case of transgression, shall be really awarded to him."

A Decree of the 30th October, 1816, also enacts— "Since experience has taught us that the bearing of assumed or invented names is injurious to the security of civil intercourse, as well as to the efficiency of the police force, we hereby order the following :—1. No one shall under pain of a fine of from five to fifty thalers, or of a proportionate imprisonment, *make use of a name which does not belong to him.* 2. If this assumption or invention of a name takes place with *intent to deceive,* the regulations of the *general penal law come into force."*

There is also a Royal Cabinet order of the 15th of April, 1822, to the effect, that no one may alter his family or general name without permission of the Sovereign. "I (The King) do not consider it necessary, on the report of the Ministry of the 27th of March, to promulgate any further decree on the unchangeableness of family or general names, but determine hereby that no one shall be allowed to alter his family or general name without permission of the Sovereign, under pain of a fine of fifty thalers or four weeks' imprisonment, even where the act does not proceed from any unlawful intention." Coll. of Laws of 1822, No. 7., S. 108.

The Law of America.

In America even, with all its lawless license, the countenance of the law was necessary to make the assumption of a name legal for social and commercial purposes. On this American question the *Spectator* says :—" In America the change requires an Act of the State Legislature ; and, to save trouble, all applications are lumped together in one schedule [and] passed as the Houses rise." June 21, 1862.

The Ancient of Scotland.

In Scotland, formerly, the false assumption of a name was equal to the false assumption of coat armour, which was punished as forgery.

Unfortunate Women compelled by law to change their Family name.

Salverte remarks, " When the system of slavery was in full force throughout the world, excess of work and privations were not the greatest of the miseries inflicted upon a sex with whom life is less precious than modesty. As soon as a woman had become the mere toy of public debauchery, it was enacted by law that she should change her name. It was taken for granted that she had only been reduced to such a state of disgrace by some kind of force, and it was not thought right that she should prostitute both her person and the name which allied her to some honourable family. The law was obeyed, even when the disgrace had been voluntarily incurred."

The Attorney-General distinctly stated the law as far as was required. He said "That people were not bound to recognise the illegal assumption of a name." If Royal license has not sanctioned an assumptive name, so the law cannot be twisted, or be made to make people accept that assumption. Here is the hitch. *The Attorney-General's opinion on the subject.*

A general rule should be enforced by the state, with legal forms which should everywhere be the same, that a change of name should be forbidden in all cases, except those in which the regular authorities permitted a change, provided it were effected with the greatest publicity; that *the assuming of a different name should be punished as a forgery."* Salverte 278. Upon a recent occasion in Parliament, reference was made as to how far it was lawful for an individual to assume a surname at pleasure. The case which was cited to favour this idea came before Sir Joseph Jekyll, in 1730, (and not 1735 as stated in the House,) when Master of the Rolls, who, in giving judgment upon the case of Barlow *v.* Bateman, (see P. Williams, 65), remarked, " I am satisfied the usage of passing Acts of Parliament for the taking upon one a surname is but modern, and that any one may take upon him what surname, and as many surnames, as he pleases, without an Act of Parliament." *Unauthorized Assumption of a name should be punished as a Forgery.* *The Master of the Rolls' decision revoked by the House of Lords.*

On reference to 4 Brown's Parl. Cases, p. 194, or to the Archœologia Papers, vol. 18, p. 111, it will be found that the decision of Sir Joseph Jekyll was reversed by the House of Lords, on what I believe to be their ancient right of prescription. The Peers said, upon their deciding the matter, " *that the individual ought to have inherited by birth, or have obtained an* AUTHORITY *for using the name."* [See the case of Leigh *v.* Leigh, reported in 15 Vesey, 92, and others there quoted.] *The opinion of the Lords upon false Assumptions of Surnames.*

D

"Free Trade" in surnames would be very detrimental to society at large. What right has any man to the property of another? A family name is an inseperably invested property.

The great question for the public to consider is this. Genealogy in name (illegally assumed), implies such in fact ; and if an abuse of this nature is once tolerated, it will eventually become a serious difficulty for that public to know " Who's who" in a few years. Genealogy in name, and Genealogy in fact, is too important a matter for society, as the custodians of their own good names, to lose sight of. An indiscriminate adoption of surnames would inflict great injustice upon those families who might unfortunately happen to have their name filched and prostituted, as has been done by Bugg, and as Iago feelingly expresses himself to Othello :—

The false Assumption of Surnames detrimental to Genealogy

> Good name in man and woman, dear my lord,
> Is the immediate jewel of their souls :
> Who steals my purse steals trash . . . .
> But he that filches from me my good name,
> Robs me of that which not enriches him,
> And makes me poor indeed.
>
> Act II. Sc. 3.

Shakespeare's estimation of a Surname.

Moreover, a license to adopt surnames at pleasure would tend to impede, if not to utterly confound, in a short time, all genealogical inquiry, in throwing grave doubts over our parish registers and other documents after a certain date, as to the identity of individuals ; because, after the second generation, the false assumption of a surname is lost sight of—it has already become an established imposture—and, in the meantime, if the impostor's family have risen to wealth and position, the armorial bearings, &c., if any belonged to the assumed name, as a matter of course follow. Now—among all old families—high and low, rich and poor, armorial bearings are oftener of more

Importance of Armorial Bearings, and their relationship with names.

importance than the surname itself. Again, (speaking
from well known instances of such gross assumption,)
there is the certainty that the descendants of the
assumer will become horse-leech claimants to blood
relationship with their supposed kinsmen, although
bastards of the worst taint, in name and fact.

CHAPTER III.

GREAT stress has been laid on the euphoniousness of aristocratic names ; of their being more pleasing to the ear and the eye ; and as implying something beyond that of common names : yet, upon inquiry, most of those ancient, royal, and aristocratic surnames—not originally local—are positively more vulgar in themselves than that of the originally honest and industrious surname of Smith, a workman, and others which are habitually slighted and jested with. What enhances the value of aristocratic names is that they have been made honourable and historically illustrious by their custodians for the time being performing deeds of valour in the field, and distinction in the cabinet, in ages past ; and, consequently, in all justice and equity, between man and man, those families alone have the sole and invested right of bearing such time-honoured surnames. This law is recognized in the law of Deeds of Patent ; then why not *patent* names in deeds also.

I will now quote an instance of the class of surnames just spoken of, and I may add that the less we know of their origin, the more we shall admire them. Some years since, a writer in Chambers' Journal gave the following legend as connected with the origin of the name " Charles," German, Karl. All freemen that were not Jarls or nobles were Karls (A-S ceorls), or commons, and this last term came of course to be one of disparagement, as we find in churl to this day. He who was afterwards Charlemagne, was brought up as the son of a miller, in ignorance of his royal parentage.

Having occasion to appear in the queen's presence, his unpolished manners offended her majesty, who ordered her courtiers to remove that *Karl* (clown) from her sight. The Karl retained the name, and made it illustrious, Karl der Grosse.

Again, when individuals are inclined to find fault with their names being uneuphonious, they ought to appease their poor weak minds with comparing their own with others, even that of royalty. The surname borne by the present dynasty of the House of Brunswick is uneuphonious to some people ; but to all, its origin is certainly the most inhuman of all known names, if history is to be believed ; yet, our beloved Queen, bears the name of Guelph with pride and honour. Who would care to bear the surname 'Vilain ?' yet it is borne by one of the most ancient houses of Europe. The Belgian patronymic of Count Vilain is venerated for its antiquity. Roger (Lacy), Constable of Chester, was surnamed " Hell " ; and how many there are of the name of " Devil "—in Europe alone, it is impossible to say.

[margin note: The surname Guelph.]

[margin note: The surnames Vilain, Hell and Devil.]

Coming now to a period nearer our own, it is remarkable that, after the conquest of this kingdom by the Normans in after times, we should possess so few purely Norman surnames, yet, what few we have (not local) were originally allusive ; we have Basset, the fat ; Giffard, the liberal ; Percy, a gross fellow ; Front-de-Boeuf, bullock's head ; and names of servitude in Marshal, Grosvenor, Butler, Stuart,* Lardiner, and Napier. Lardiner, is one whose duty it is to attend to the provisions in the royal larder on the coronation day. The last name sails under very false colours in its derivation, it means, according to the ancient rolls, the guardian of the napery or table cloths used at the royal table. We entertain a very erroneous idea on

[margin note: Norman French personal Names and Names of servitude.]

* Only so spelt after the return of Mary Queen of Scots from France

the derivation of the surname Hussey, it is not a name of contempt, but a Norman French name for holly tree.

I am only aware of two surnames, as alluding to personal defects, among the Norman nobles, and those were given to John, the son of Serlo, the founder of Knaresbro' Castle, who was called Monoculus, one-eyed, and Baron Maureward, or the squinter.

Old English Names of contempt. Among our old English surnames many are of contempt, as Goff and Strutt, both mean a fool. The latin *Stultus* a fool, becomes in German *Stolz* a proud man, and in English Stout ; Seymour, a seamer or tailor ; Leicester, a weaver ; Trollope, a slattern ; Parnell and Puttick denote immodest women; Wiggles, the owner of a diseased neck ; Card and Caird, a tinker ; Maunder, a beggar ; Lavander and Lavator, a washerman ; Shelley, a winkle ; Chaucer, a name given to a peculiar kind of boot-maker.

Howard, an ancient official name of warfare. The surname Howard does not imply *Swineherd*, but is a name of much more honourable distinction. The illustrious Camden says that it means "highwarden," but of what he has not stated. The origin may be "high-warden" of the Hog Standard, as it is of a similar class to that of the British surname of office "Pendragon," and also to that of "Durward"— doorkeeper. Among many of the British tribes, the hog was a favourite war ensign, presented in an image of bronze, and which was fastened to the head of the staff, similar, precisely, to that of the Roman eagle. Diodorus thus alludes to it, "Some carried the shapes of beasts in brass," (B. V. C. 2.) and Worsaae notes that among the Gauls the hog was a sacred animal, and is represented on old coins. The Howard family may be descendants of some of the leaders of the latest British tribes, as they are known to have been in England long before the conquest.

Gaelic defective names. Among Gaelic aristocratic surnames we find such as Campbell (Cam-pal), crooked-mouth ; Cameron, crooked-nose ; Camoys, snub-nose ; among the democratic is that of Mac Clellan, the son of the bastard. The Conqueror as a proud man styled himself in one of his first proclamations, " I, William, surnamed the Bastard."

CHAPTER IV.

THERE ever has been, and must continue to be, some interest attached to a name ; now, as every man has a name, so every man must feel some curiosity to know of what that name is significant, and how it originated, in fact the history of his name ; this acquaintanceship is not unattainable. It would have been well for the Buggs and Buggeys had they adopted such a plan, and not have exposed themselves in the manner they have done.

I can see no cause to object to the possessors of ugly surnames, (which may be such now, but were not so formerly), resuming the earliest, or an early mode of spelling their names, to divest them of their ugliness.

I hold that a family name is a venerable historical fact, indentifying and connecting the present generation, with their ancestors, whose only monument that name is, and as such, it becomes them as honest men—men of mature and staid minds, to hold that name sacred. Is it nothing to be connected with the history of one's country, and to feel—

> " The name of every noble ancestor
> A bond upon your soul against disgrace ?"

It is much to feel, that the high and the honourable belong to a name that is pledged to the present by recollections of the past.

This matter becomes of greater importance when we consider that the possessors of poor but honest names, possess a lineage of unbroken descent, and to more fully illustrate this point, I will quote a passage from Mr. Disraeli in testimony of this statement, he gives more than one example in illustration :— "'Ancient lineage!'" said Mr. Millbank: a great authority on Genealogy. " I never heard of a peer with an ancient lineage. The real old family of this country are to be found *among the peasantry*, the gentry, too, may lay some claim to old blood. I can point you out some Saxon families in this country who can trace their pedigrees beyond the conquest. I know of some Norman gentlemen whose fathers undoubtedly came over with the Conqueror. " But a peer with an ancient lineage is to me quite a novelty."

Mr. Millbank's statement is fully realized in certain noble families, who have assumed the surnames attached to their created title, which surnames are considered inherent to those titles, and, are so assumed in consequence of their consanguinity, which will be seen in the following list of nobles. The Duke of Wellington was not a Wellesley, but a Colley, whose armorials bearings he bore ; his grandfather, Richard Colley, assumed the relative Wesley, since euphonised into Wellesley, which name the Iron Duke literally *made.* Another branch of the family still retain the name of Colley, slightly altered as that of Earl Cowley. The Duke of Northumberland is not a Percy but a Smithson, his ancestor, Sir Hugh Smithson, having received the honours of the house of Percy, because his wife's grandmother was a Percy. Lord Clarendon is not a Hyde, Lord Strafford is not a Wentworth, Lord Dacre is a Trevor, Lord Wilton is not an Egerton but a Grosvenor, Lord de Tabley is not a Warren but a Leicester ; Earl Nelson is a Bolton, his grandfather was Thomas Bolton, his grandmother the great Nelson's sister. Lord Anglesea is not a Paget but a Bayley, the Duke of Marlborough is not a Churchill but a Spenser : in short, one might almost go through the entire peerage to the same end.

Certain titled Nobles not such in lineage, but by names of Assumption.

E

The Athenæum very judiciously remarks, in speaking of individuals and their surnames, that " Their names are their own, acquired by inheritance, like any other property they may possess, and a very important part of their social history ; as such, a proud man would as soon part with his name as with his character, his genius, and his blood." I will but cite another writer's opinion on this important subject.

He is himself the possessor of an ugly name, and very plainly tells his tale through the columns of *The Times*, 6th January last. He says, " He rejoices in a not very euphonius surname, of which he is proud on account of its antiquity, respectability, and, above all, on account of its rarity. Is not the rarity of my name a sort of property vested in me and mine ? And am I to be shorn of that attribute ? If I and the other ———'s have been ever touchy and sensitive to the honour of the ——— name, what becomes of that good and useful feeling if the name may be at the service of every blackguard who finds it convenient to assume an *alias*." He adds, "If names are to be shaken off for a mere whim, at least shield families from the discomfort of having their names appropriated by men who have no motive to keep them untarnished." Have we not frequently known and read of individuals addressing the public through the press, stating that they were not the Mr. So-and-so who had committed himself.

If a name denoting worth, integrity, and honour has a commercial value, quite as much so has it a value in social life ; the same principle holds good in both ; hence the necessity for a law to restrain unprincipled persons from stealing a name.

As regards names, our Celtic ancestors did not consider that they laboured under any disadvantages in having ugly surnames. They distinguished each other by names strictly characteristic of the bearer through personal defects and eccentric peculiarities : as Doity, saucy ; Douce, wise ; Doylt, stupid. Nay, had the cognomen Bug, and the man—the great man of Wakefield—been then in existence, he would pro-bably have been known as the real original Humbug.

The Anglo-Saxons were very indifferent givers of surnames ; about the year 800 we find the names of Aethelwerde Stameran—the stammerer : Godwine Dreflan—the driveller ; they made little or no use of scripture names, John, Thomas, &c., so that their christian names are extremely numerous, which occasions them at times to be taken for surnames, much more so than ours ; and they seldom called a son by the name of his father, as it caused confusion of persons—which they particularly guarded against, but when they did do so they gave another (additional) name peculiar to the person, besides that of descent or the surname, which Camden notes—(and cites William of Malmesbury)—as the son of Edmund was called Edmund*ing*, which with us is called Edmund-*son*; Edgar—Edgar*ing*—Edgar*son*, &c.—Rem. p. 106.

Some old Norse names are noteworthy if only for their comicality. King Canute's father, King Svend, was surnamed Treskjæg—Splitbeard ; this name I fancy, if given now for the same peculiarity, would make it more common than that of Smith, Brown and Jones if all put together. King Harald—sur-named Blaatand—blue-tooth, from a defective tooth. King Eric, surnamed Blod Oxe, from his strength of arm and irresistible prowess in wielding his battle axe. Ivar Beenlese—boneless, probably a gymnast, or from his suppleness of body. *Thorketil*—Myrehoved,—ant-head, from the peculiarity of his facial organs, and their resemblance to that insect. Halfdan, sur-named Scarpæ—the sharper. Berne and Urse—bears of men : and Miss Ursula really means " little she-bear."

Accidental events concurring with names. Names—at times are strange things in their concurring with accidental events; among such may be classed the names of Huss and Luther. At the martyrdom of John Huss (goose), he predicted " They burn a goose, but in a hundred years a swan will arise out of the ashes." The name Luther signifies swan.

Had it not been for Constantine's happy and fortuitous name, he never would have been raised from the ranks to rule the empire. Servants occasionally make sad mistakes in announcing names ; such a mishap befell a certain Mr. Delaflete, in London. From his indistinct mode of pronouncing his name, the porter understood it to be *Delaflote*, and so proclaimed it to the footman in waiting, who some how or other mistook the initial letter of the name, and the luckless visitor, a quiet, shy, reserved young man, was actually ushered into the midst of a crowded drawing-room by the ominous appellation of Mr. Hell-a-flote.

Mr. Lower in his work on " English Surnames," gives a curious example of the combining of two names,—he says " One of the most singular designations I ever met with is that of a gentleman of fortune. His name was Bear, and as he had maternal relatives of the name of Savage, his parents gave him the christian (or rather unchristian) name of Savage ! Hence he enjoyed the pleasing and amiable name of Savage Bear, Esq. ! !

Transition of European Surnames. From about the year 1410 to 1600 the translation of surnames from the vulgar to a classical tongue was quite the rage among the learned men of Europe. In England, this irregularity called forth an Act entitled the Statute of Additions (1 Henry V., c. 5), to fix surnames, &c.* This transition of sur-

* In the fourth year of the reign of Edward IV., an Act was passed entitled—" At the request of the Commons, it is ordained and established by authority of the said Parliament, [holden at

names probably first drew Camden's attention to
the subject of surnames ; their origin and derivation in a collected form. It afforded our "nourice
of antiquity" more real pleasure than any other
in the study of archæology, we find him strik-
ing into etymological subjects when deeply en-
gaged on matters of greater importance. In his
" Remaines " he notices some few of the following
very ugly names, amongst the most illustrious Roman
families.

He says,—" If you please to compare the Roman
names that seeme so stately, because you understand
them not, you will disdaine them in respect of our
meanest names." Many of their proper surnames
were derived from mean and frivolous circumstances,
yet they and their descendants bore them with honour.

What is Galba, but maggot, (according to Seu-
tonius ;) Fronto, but beetle-browed ; Plautus, flat-
footed ; Crassus, fat ; Coesius, cat's eyes ; Paetus,
pink-eyed ; Cocles, with us would be Mr. One-eye ;
Claudius, Mr. Limper ; Capeto, Mr. Big-head ; (such
probably, is the correct signification of Hugh Capet's
name). Calvus, bald-pate, its equivalent in English
is Caffin, in French, Calvin ; Furius, raving ; Silo,
ape's-nose; Ancus, crooked-arm; Brutus, Mr. Stupid;
Flaccus, flap-eared ; Pandi, Mr. Bandy-legs ; Varus,
bow-legs ; Scauri, club-foots ; Pedo, was Mr. Long-
shanks ; Calous, broad-pate ; Crispus, curl-pate ;
Labeo, blabber-lip ; Chilo, flat-lips ; the Marcelli,
were hammer-heads ; the immortal Ovid, surnamed

Roman names of contempt, yet honourable in themselves

Trim in 1465], that every Irishman that dwells betwixt or amongst
Englishmen in the County of Dublin, Myeth, Ureill, and Kildare,
shall go like to an Englishman in apparel and shaving of his beard
above the mouth, ... *and shall take to him an English surname of a town,* . . . . *or colour,* . . . . *or art or science,* . . . . .
or office, ... *and that he and his issue shall use this name,*
under pain of forfeiting of his goods yearly till the premises be
done." Statutes at Large in Ireland, 1786, vol. i., p. 29.

Naso, was Mr. Nosey, or bottle-nose ; whether from its formation, or its anti-teetotalism, we have no authority to say ; and a name already familiar to the reader, Strabo, Mr. Squintum. These names are absolutely contemptible of themselves, nevertheless, they are beautiful in their associations—"worth, valour, genius, learning, have converted syllables into proverbs, and words into histories."

Roman agricultural Surnames.

Marcus Tullius, when he became a first-class grower of vetches, was honoured with the name of Cicero, a name which he immortalized more through literature than agriculture ; the latter is specially honoured in that of the Emperor Agricola. The illustrious Fabius derived his name from being an excellent grower of kidney beans. Piso, with us would be known as Mr. Pease-cod-man ; this surname would doubtless put Lord Dundreary in a quandary, being a compound containing sufficient designations to satisfy any three Britons in or out of Parliament. These are comparatively simple and inoffensive names as compared with others of a more personal and opprobrious nature.

Roman opprobrious Surnames.

Archdeacon Nares, remarks in his " Heraldic Anomalies,"—" We should think Ass and Sow not very elegant names, yet the Cornelian and Tremellean families obtained them." Contemptuous names were given of a man's calling, the Bubulic, from a cow-herd ; the Porci, from a hog-butcher ; the Suilli were descended from a swine-herd ; its equivalent in the British tongue is Grice. Personal peculiarities and afflictive defects of the person, were symbolized in the name, and were, in fact, defective names, as Balbus, the stutterer ; Louis, the second son of Charlemagne, was surnamed Balbus.

Origin of the Popes changing their names.

The origin of the custom of the Popes changing their names after their election to the papacy—according to Camden, who quotes Platina, the Roman ecclesiastical writer—was exactly the same as that which

influenced Bugg and Buggey of our day, disgust of
an ugly name. A cardinal being elected whose proper
name signified Swine-snout, (which, by general consent, being deemed unseemly for such a dignity,) it
was changed to Sergius (2nd).

The Italians of the present day are not a wit more
courteous than their ancestors, in the names they give
to some families, as for instance—Malatesta, chuckle-
head ; Boccanigras, black-muzzle ; Gozzi, chubby-
chops.

The surname Servius, according to Salverte, does
not signify *born in slavery*, as Camden states, (Rem. p.
105,) but that of a child whose mother died in giving
him birth.

Vital
errors as to
the correct
meaning
of certain
Roman
names.

A similar misconception occurs in the name
Spurius, which is supposed to signify illegitimate
descent, whereas it really means a sower. Plutarch
observes that this mistake arose through the Romans
using the abbreviation S. P. for Spurius, and also for
the words *sine patre* (without father). In fact, further evidence can be shown proving the above to be
the truth. We are all aware that divorce was allowed
in ancient Rome, yet it was 523 years before any person availed himself of it : and, strange to say, the first
individual who did so (if we are to believe history)
was *Spurius* Carbilius Ruga, a man passionately fond
of his wife. Now, we of the present day have no right
to judge the parent of this Roman of a breach of the
seventh commandment, seeing that this statement is
recognised by ancient and modern historians as a
positive fact. But should there be any doubt as to
the legitimacy of the name and person, we have only
to remember *Spurius* Fusius, who was the first
herald that ever was created among the Romans, in
the war which Tullius Hostilius waged against the old
Latins ; he had the official name of Pater Patratus,
the chief of the heralds. It was necessary that the

candidate chosen to fill this office should be married and have children ; and, further, it was absolutely essential to his election that his father should be then living, which distinctly disproves the statements of some ancient authors, who assert that the name signifies illegitimacy. Thus we find the same absurd idea prevailing among ancient authors with regard to certain supposed ugly names, as at the present time exists among the old Buggs and little Buggeys, all arising from the want of a proper understanding of the derivation of such like names.

CHAPTER V.

WITH regard to names denoting personal defects, "John-with-a-Squint" was cited in the House of Commons as being a nickname of contempt. Of course the House naturally enough laughed at this instance of modern nomenclature. Probably the originators of that laugh had not in their mind's eye the immortal Strabo. The historic surname of the great geographer would be with us Mr. Squintum, yet that illustrious man saw no just reason to change his honoured name. Among the names of ancient Persia we find that of the justly celebrated Barasmanes, the squinter, and opponent of Belisarius. Again, in the Conqueror's train, we find an individual noble who revelled in the surname "Maureward," or squinter. Consequently, "John-with-a-Squint" is really a very fine" name. Names of reproach, contempt, and ignominy, have been in existence since the men of Babel said one to another "let us make us a name."

A modern English nickname.

An ancient classical nickname as a Surname.

What is the Hebrew name, *Caleb*; the Persian, *Cyrus*; the Teutonic, *Guelph*; and the English, *Machell*; but nicknames, originally, of certain persons likened and named after evil or rabid *dogs*?

Universality of Nicknames of one class.

Nazarines, was first contemptuously applied to Christians by the Jews, (Acts xxiv. 5,) and from them taken up by the heathen, who also called them *Galileans*. The Emperor Julian published an edict forbidding them to be called by any other name than that of Galileans, hoping thereby to banish the use of the title Christians. St. Jerome says that whenever a Christian was seen passing in the streets, the people would cry out "*behold a Greek impostor*."

Nicknames of the Early Christians.

F

The term "Greek" a vile Nickname.

They were also called *impostors*, and *Greeks.* Gibbons says in his "Decline and Fall," A.D. 527-565 :—" Under the command of Belisarius, the subjects of Justinian often deserved to be called Romans, but the unwarlike appellation of *Greeks* was imposed as a term of reproach by the haughty Goths." The Irish are nicknamed Grecians, and the natives anciently were first known by the name Iris, a pure Egyptian word.

The title Dominus originally a Nickname.

The ancient title of *Dominus* appeared at first so abominably insolent as a modified nickname, that the Emperors Augustus and Tiberius would not allow it to be given to themselves. The senseless Caligula first assumed it. Shortly after, it was given not only to emperors, but likewise to all governors and many courtiers. In France it was long given only to kings. In England, Dominus was long used only of God and the King. At length it became common to all noblemen. It became abbreviated in time to " Dom," then corrupted to " Dan," and is so used by Chaucer. It is also found corrupted into " Dam," for the male ; and " Dame," for the female. The former has long been obsolete as a name of honour, but as a surname it is still in being in Herefordshire ; but the latter is still used in France—hence, " Madame" (my Lady) ; English, Madam.

In the seventeenth century, the epithet MISS, applied to females, was considered a term of vile reproach, the name being that by which females of a certain class were usually designated. *Mistress*, in contradistinction, then meant a sweetheart, or one that a man was courting for his wife. (Haydn.)

The origin of the terms Whig and Tory.

According to De Foe (Review vii., 296-7), the origin of the term " Tory, is Irish, and was first made use of there in the time of Queen Elizabeth's wars in Ireland. It signified a kind of robber, who, being *listed* in neither army, preyed in general upon the

country, without distinction of English or Spaniard.
In England, the real godfather of the name was Titus
Oates ; he called every man a Tory that opposed
him in discourse, till at last the word Tory became
popular. As to the word Whig, it is Scots. The use of
it began there when the western men, called Camero-
nians, took arms frequently for their religion.   These
men, about the year 1681, took up arms, and caused
the famous insurrection at Bothwell bridge.   The
Duke of Monmouth, then in favour, was sent against
them by King Charles II., and defeated them. At his
return, instead of thanks for the good service, he
found himself ill-treated for using them too merci-
fully ; and the Duke of Lauderdale told King Charles,
with an oath, that the Duke had been so civil to the
Whigs, because he was a Whig himself in his heart.
This made it a court word ; and in a little while all
the friends and followers of the Duke were called
Whigs.''

PART II.

CHAPTER I.

Probable cause of the disgust of Bugg & Buggey with their Surnames. THERE cannot be a doubt that the immortal and facetious Tom Hood is to be blamed for having humbugged the Buggs and the Buggeys out of their odd surnames. He has said :—

> A name ! If the party had a voice
> What mortal would be a Bug by choice ?"

Although the name is so, it bears not the remotest affinity to "a familiar beast and a friend to man."

Conjecture as to the meaning of Bugg. Eminent philologists have noticed this comical name, Bugg. First, Mr. Kemble, in his work on *Anglo-Saxon Surnames*, mentions an A-S, lady and an Abbess, who bore the name HROTHWRAN BUCGE. Second, Mr. Ferguson, in his *English Surnames*, thinks that "it is a name of reverence rather than of contempt, derived from a root implying bowed or bent." Mr. Lower, in his *Patronymica Britannica*, believes it to be "of the same origin as Bogue," but what that means he has forgot to state. However, the two names Bugg and Buggey, in my opinion, are both ancient and honourable ; and were either of them my born inheritance to-day, I would not part with it for the choice of the names "of all the Howards," with that of Norfolk "to boot."

Accordingly, I can fully appreciate Mr. Buggey, the coachbuilder's reason for giving his name to a peculiar description of vehicle. As an armorial painter, he evidently was fully alive to the origin and honourable meaning of his name, and hence his endeavour to perpetuate it in the *Buggey* cab. A certain Mr. Buggey's exultation in his Surname.

With all due deference to Mr. Buggey, of Bedford, he is certainly very much to blame for ever troubling the public with his imaginary (hereditary) wrongs, (or thin-skinnedness). It would have been more to the purpose had he set to work when a youth, and not so flourishing, and ferreted out the original and implied meaning of his name, instead of brooding over its euphony as he says he has done. Could but Juliet have whispered in his ear, " What's in a name," all might now have been well with him, and he, truly speaking, a proud *New-man*, revelling in a time and deed-honoured name, won by the blood of his fathers, under the banner of the premier Baron of England, on the plains of France. Now—he can but say with Argyle, " I cannot call these my own." For why ? Because he has forsaken the name—the symbol of his ancestors ! Contrast the acts of the two Mr. Buggeys : the man of letters shakes off his patronymic as he would an old shoe ; but the gentleman coachbuilder, who was a true type of his forefathers, gloried in and perpetuated that patronymic. Such manifest ignorance of family history is to be sincerely and deeply deplored, especially so in an old county (Beds.) family like that of Buggey. Yet, there is one redeeming feature in his assumption of the name Newman ; it is his maternally ; consequently, he claims it by birthright, and by the ancient law of custom, which makes it strictly legal. Yet, withal, he is a vain, and not a proud man ; hence, probably, the change of name.

But the assumption of a name which a person has

no right to is a serious matter ; one which the whole community ought most emphatically to protest against. It is an intolerable "encroachment on the rights of others."

The gross and audacious assumption of such a time-honoured name as that of Howard of Norfolk, *reversed*, is inexcusable. A name which it has taken centuries to make what it is, and many precious lives to build up, in serving the common weal, truly belongs to the British nation.

As Hector said, so the Howards have done : —

> " Let me be foremost to defend the throne,
> And guard my father's glories, and my own."

The historic associations of the name are too honourable and too great to be prostituted in such a vile manner, by a pretender falsely styling himself " Norfolk Howard." Why should we for a moment permit any daring upstart to assume a name which he has clearly shown himself so utterly unworthy to bear?

> " Where now in *Hector* shall we Hector find ?
> *A manly form, without a manly mind.*
> Is this, O chief ! a hero's boasted fame ?
> *How vain, without the merit, is the name !*"
>
> IL. B. xvii. 155.

The Assumption of Historical State Names forbidden among the Romans. The Romans would not tolerate such an assumption, for we read that " Valerius and Horatius thought it peculiarly their duty to oppose the Decemviri in their *iniquitous* endeavours to assume the same names as men (Valerii and Horatii) who had heretofore signalized themselves."

Pensions, orders, and titles were small things in comparison with an honourable and laudatory surname ; admitted to be a just one by public opinion, **The same among the Athenians.** "in those fortunate days when not a dishonest man could be found." (Cicero.) In Athens, where that same feeling was dignified by a principle of gratitude, it led to the passing of a law, which enacted " that no slave should bear the name of either Aristogeiton or Harmodius, lest the memory of those brave champions of their country's liberty should be tarnished by any *lower association.*" Thus we find, in pagan Rome and Athens, the same vain-glorious hankering after honoured names which we experience at the present day.

If the head of a family possesses an indelicate, but not an historic surname, and he is determined that his issue shall bear another, let that other be the maternal, it is his children's birthright; either by itself, or as a compound prefixed to the paternal. We are not the descendants of the Athenians of old, who passed a law by which it was forbidden to give a child its mother's name ; but rather of the Romans, who perpetuated the mother's maiden name through one of her children: and this ancient custom has of late gained considerable estimation among us. In fact, with a certain class of people—those who dabble a little in family genealogy, it is an essential point to give the mother's maiden name to the eldest born male: if to one, let it be given to all, under the circumstances named. In the person of Sir Edward G. *Lytton* Bulwer *Lytton*, we find the same name used as a Christian and a surname, the first being that of baptism and the second of circumstance. Sir Edward assumed the surname Lytton in 1841, on succeeding to the estate of Knebworth, Herts., by the death of his mother, the heiress of the Lyttons.

A mode suggested for the alteration of an ugly Surname.

Now, supposing the great Bugg had named a Mary Dunstan, and followed the suggestion as here stated, their issue would be named Dunstan-Bugg, thus effectually nullifying the ugliness of the name, and destroying the supposed zoological kinship, yet not dis-associating a name of marked antiquity.

This rule of connection, from of yore, has been in existence in Armoury, where the husband bears the arms of his wife ; then why not the rule be also applied to surnames ?

The desirability of a husband taking upon himself his wife's name.

M. Salverte very applicably thus puts the question :—" Pride connects the armorial bearings of the husband and the wife in the same shield ; why should not affection unite their names ? When the wife takes her husband's name, why does not the husband join her name to his own ? The custom is a common one in Geneva, and in many provinces of France. The law might sanction it, and make its use general. A prænomen placed before the family name would designate a bachelor : two family names joined together would indicate one who had been married.............. There would be that of having a constant standing memorial of the name of the particular family from which the husband had had the honour of selecting a suitable companion. p.p. 256-7.

The Assumption of a Mother's name.

Some of our ancient nobles took their mother's surname—as Geoffrey Fitz-Maldred took the name of Neville, whose descendants have since made it nationally historic. The latest instance of this class of assumptions through relationship, to be found among those of historic fame of the present day, is that of the illustrious Lord Clyde. Sir Colin Campbell was born a McLiver, (that being his father's name,) but family circumstances led to the adoption of the maternal surname—Campbell.

The first William de Percy of England was surnamed Gernon, or Algernon—whiskers—about 1080.

Assumption of a Wife's name.

His great-grand-daughter, Agnes, was co-heir to her brother William. She would only consent to marry Josceline de Louvaine, son of Godfrey, Duke of Brabant, and brother to Alice, second Queen of Henry I. upon condition that he would assume either the name or armorials of Percy, relinquishing his own. His sister, the Queen, advised him to assume the name, retaining the arms of his father's principality, showing his relationship, should that dukedom ever become extinct ; and hence the origin of the title (of Lord) Louvaine in the Percy family.

CHAPTER II.

JULIET'S query of "What's Montacute" or Montague, is exceedingly apropos to the present inquiry. It is a name which in some measure shews the early origin of a certain class of historical surnames—device names, or names derived from the armorial achievements of their first possessors, and which are of great interest—not only to the antiquary and the historian, but should also be so to the lover of Shakespeare. Notwithstanding Juliet's insinuation and apparent indifference regarding a name and its meaning,—signified in her query of "What's in a name," she yet admits that one is necessary, and it is certainly very singular that the surname on which her ladyship is pleased to cavil, is of that very class of designations which has of late attracted so much attention.

Armoury, its use in the derivation of names. Armoury, miscalled Heraldry, has facetiously been dubbed as "The Science of fools with long memories." To those unacquainted with its beauties, it will certainly appear so : yet it is a study by which family history and relationship can be proved better than by surname. For its antiquity as connecting a person with his name and device, we have only to So used by the ancient Egyptians. refer to Herodotus, who says, in speaking of the Egyptians, that "Each person has a seal-ring, and a cane, or walking-stick, on the top of which is carved an apple, a rose, a lily, an eagle, or some figure or other, for to have a stick without a device is unlawful." B. I. (CLIO.) 195. There can be but little doubt that these and other emblems were recognised among the higher grade of Egyptians, as family or personal badges of cognisance.

Of the period when the use of armoury was
in its greatest repute in England, no person dared to
assume any device or bearing without the authority
of the Earl-Marshal, or his Kings-at-Arms. "Any
individual who presumed, by assumption, to offend
the laws of the court of honour, were liable to heavy
fines and personal duresse, which in many instances
have been rigidly enforced."*

Among the Normans, anterior to the conquest, and
till the reign of Edward I., it was the fashion to sym-
bolize the names of noble families from their armorial
bearings, or *armes-parlantes*, these device-names are of
much greater antiquity than name-devices, or canting-
arms.

Mons. Salverte, in his "History of Surnames,"
when speaking of emblems or armorial bearings at the

*Norman
device-
names.*

* The right of bearing arms was in those days of such esteem,
that the celebrated and long contest between Edward Hastings and
Reginald Grey for bearing the arms of the family of the former,
Or, a Manche Gules, lasted little less than twenty years, in the court-
military, before the Constable and Marshal of England, wherein,
after a great expenditure of money, Edward Hastings, the chal-
lenger, and heir-male of the family, was not only condemned in
£970 17s. 10d. (the money of that period—equalling some
£15,000 of ours), with all costs, (Grey swearing that he had spent
a thousand marks more £29,000, and the arms granted to Grey;
but imprisoned sixteen years for disobeying that sentence. 2 H. 4.

King James 1. imprisoned a herald for granting a Coat of Arms
then in being, to another.

I am informed by James Stockdale, Esq., of Carke House,
Cartmel, that "a Mr. W. Garrat of Garrat Houses, near Cartmel,
was a master mason, he cut most of the arms on the tombstones in
Cartmel church-yard, and in the church some hundred years ago.
He made his own monument, and after his death it was placed near
the vestry door, in Cartmel church. He assumed the arms of a
local family, named Towers, "on a chevron between three towers,
as many pellats;" and so cut them on his shield. A Herald came
down on business or pleasure, and cut a piece with a chisel out of
the shield, or rather cut away the three towers &c., which were in
relief."

period of the crusades, says—" Those lords . . . could be recognised in the emblems painted upon their shields and their banners, stirring emblems, which were almost worshipped by their retainers." Vol. I. p. 183.

The necessity of retaining Devices as Names, as done by the Ancient Egyptians. At tournaments, or in battle, a Knight used to present himself with closed visor ; none knew him otherwise than by the symbol he wore. Hence that sign became a designation, or true surname, which was never allowed to be lost when once some glorious achievement had been associated with it. History tells us expressly that during the era of the Norman Kings, many of the crusader chiefs attached the symbols they had adopted in the East to the whole of their family, till the names derived from these symbols became like the symbols themselves—permanent and hereditary. Such is the origin of device-names, and it is quite natural that arms should have to do with names ; for the names clearly proceed from the arms, as armorial devices.

Armorial bearings as Surnames on Tombs. On ancient table-tombs, in churches, there are generally no inscriptions. The arms on the effigies were quite sufficient to show of what family the person represented by the effigy was.

Feudal Chiefs granted part of their Armorials to their Retainers as Names. Mr. Planché, in his " Pursuivant of Arms," p. 66, says :—" Anciently......every feudal chief granted or conceded a portion of his own armorial bearings to favoured followers in battle, or holders of land under them." Such, then, in my humble opinion, is the true origin of the honourable Norman names, Buggey and Bugg.

CHAPTER III.

I HAVE already alluded to the rarity of Norman names, but now it is necessary to mention that of Roger di Buci, Bugey, or Busli, who came to England with the Conqueror ; and I have little doubt that he had been connected somehow with the lordship of Bugey, in Normandy.

The first Bugey in England.

This Roger de Buci, or Bugey, was intimately connected with the county of Lancaster. He held, conjointly with Aubert de Grelle, the entire hundred of Blackburnshire, and the Royal Barony of Penwortham—Preston. The name is here oftener written Busli. He had two brothers, Warin and Richard. The first appears to have acted in Lancashire as his deputy ; consequently, he is frequently styled Baron of Penwortham, which he ultimately became. He was a *"sair saint"* to Preston and its neighbourhood, but a great benefactor to the abbey of Evesham, Worcestershire, to which he gave the priory of Penwortham. Richard de Buci gave a carucate of land, in Rufford, to St. Werburgh's, in Chester.

His connection with Lancashire.

Roger de Bugey's Yorkshire estates consisted of 55 manors, and part of the Honour of Tickhill, in which was included the Barony of Wartre ; and in nine other counties he held over 300 manors.

His estates

By some means unknown to us, the Barony of Wartre passed from Roger de Bugey to the Trusbut family, who appear to have been settled there from the Danish occupation. De Bugey's armorial bearings were *three water bougets*, probably adopted by him in memory of some hardship during the first crusade. These bearings have always been considered to have

His Armorial Bearings.

originated in the Trusbut family, because they bore "*Trois Boutz* d'eau ;" whereas it is but the earliest mode of *canting* spelling, and pointing with undoubted certainty to its "Frenchified" origin. Trusbut is a device name adopted from the feudal Baron's armorials. They assumed the bearings of De Buci as tenants in feu, which was then customary.

Variations of the Name. From what I have been able to make of the name it seems to have puzzled the possessors how to spell it correctly, some entertained a Grecian idea on the subject ; they looked upon polysyllabic names as "more noble and honourable" than shorter ones. I find the name written in about thirty different ways ; as Buci, Bugey, Bugi, Boci, Bogge, Busli, Busse, Buzzy, Boge, Buggey, Bussey, Bogg, Boag, Bogue, Beucey, Bucey, Bucy, Bushell, Bussoll, Boogie, Buggy, Buggie, Buxly, Busly, Borici, Bukie, Bouky, and in one case I find it with a real aristocratic handle "Le Bowge," or *the bug*, if we are to adopt the associated ideas of the descendants of these families. In Warrington and its vicinity I have found the name Buci (Bewsey) written in eleven different ways, and all different to any of the above forms. In Edinburgh the

Origin and meaning of Bugg and Buggey. same name is written differently again, Boog and Boogie. The armorial bearings borne by the Barons de Bugey, are also given to the Buggeys and Buggs. The name may have been taken from the Baron direct, or his armorial bearings, the latter is my idea, inasmuch as another and a later feudal family bore them, to whom the Buggeys were retainers, or tenants in feu.

Buggey is the old English pronunciation of the Norman-French armorial term Bouget, and Bugg, Boog, &c., are but diminitives or contractions of the same. The old French term "Bougette" a little purse, is immortalised in the political and financial world under the title of Budget. It is also to be found in water *bucket*.

The earliest instances of device-names, are to be found only after the first Crusade ; but whether Roger de Bugey took his name from his bearings, or from Bugey lordship, is uncertain. We know this, that the first *Molineux* bore a " cross *moline or*" the same being the device of his native town of Moulins, in Normandy. However, we cannot go far wrong if we only conjecture that he did. Hugh *Lupus*, the first Norman Earl of Chester, and nephew to the conqueror, bore a wolf's head couped, on his shield, and there are at the present time, several Spanish families named Lopez, bearing the wolf. The Earls Fortescue, from *forte-scue*. The *Clares* Earls of Gloucester, bore three *clarions*. *Ferriers*, the Norman Earls of Derby, bore six horse-shoes. Walter, Earl of Pembroke, and Lord *Marshal*, bore the same. *Vere*, Earl of Oxford, emblazoned a *bear*, (latin Verres). Gilbert de *Acquila* (Eagle) bore three *eagles*. Ivo de *Heriz* (Harris), three *hedgehogs*, *haris* being the French name for a hedgehog. The Lucys, ancient Barons of Cumberland, bore three lucies (pikes). The Viponts or Vipounts, afterwards altered to Veteriponts, Barons in chief of Westmoreland, and hereditary sheriffs of that county, bore six circular spots on their shield, devising their surname VI-ponts, and from which device, or single spot, we have the English surname, Roundell, and the French, Rondeau. The arms of the Viponts are now borne by the Earl of Lonsdale, his ancestors, (the Lowthers) from a very early period having been the chief retainers of those great Barons in that county. The Leibournes, another baronial family of Cumberland, bore six lions or lionells. The ancient and honourable Danish family of Machell, or Mauchael, bear three wolf-dogs courant. Roger, a cadet of that family, who was Vice-Chancellor to Richard I., styled himself Malus Catalus, *mischievous whelp ;* he bore a wolf-dog on his shield, and used the same device for his seal. At the period of the Conqueror's survey, Machell's family were located in Lonsdale, North Lancashire. His direct lineal male issue are still to be found in the same district ; moreover, it is the only family in Lancashire, if not in many other counties, which bears that high and honourable distinction of being named in Domboc.

Az. a Cross, *Moline Or*, are the arms of the ancient local family of De Molines, or Molyneux, Earls of Sefton. This description of cross is termed by Upton, an early English armorist, a cross-miller, and is a bearing alluding to the name, as William des Molines—William of the Mills—from which the town Moulins takes its name. The names of the towns Sheffield and Derby are shown in their devices, as many others in Britain are : and also the port of Antwerp, and the names Leon and Castile, in Spain ; and Berne, in Switzerland ; thus showing the general application of armory to names of persons and places.

Molineux, of Sefton, and the Armorial Bearings of the Borough of Salford. The historical associations of the Molineux family with Salford, as mistress of that hundred, have been beautifully symbolized by the heralds in the armorials of that borough, under the appropriation of the two Mill-rinds, or fer-de-Molines, on a chief. Upon reference to ancient authorities we find that the Molyneux family, during the 14th century, bore Az. a fer-de Moline or. " What's Montagu ?" It is also symbolical. Rothschild signifies, in Teutonic, Redshield. The following names have all originally been derived from armorial bearings as device names :— Trappes, Barry, Paly, Shield, Gyronny, Fess, Griffin, Lys, Chevron, Milne, Brock, Corbet, Biassets.

Canting Arms. Racine. But with regard to names giving arms, we have many very laughable incidents. M. Salverte gives the following :—" In allusion to their name, the Racines had originally placed in their coat of arms a rat and a young swan (Rat-Cygne.) The writer of

Athalie retained the swan only, because the rat offended his taste.

Many have supposed that the ancient and honourable name of "Bacon" had relationship to swine's flesh. The supposition is quite foreign to the fact: a greater injustice could scarcely have been done the scientific friar, and the philosophic lord, than that of ignoring the correct derivation of their good name. The old Saxon antiquary, Verstegans, thus states the signification :—Bacon, of the *beechen* tree, anciently called *bucon*; and, whereas, swine's flesh is now called by the name of *bacon*, it grew only at the first into such as were fatted with *bucon*, or *beech-mast* C. ix. p. 299. From Collins' Baronage we learn that the first assumer of this name was one William, a Knight, during the reign of Richard I.; his armorials were allusive to his name—Ar. a beech tree, ppr. The surnames Breakspeare and Shakespeare are evidently allusive to some deeds of valour executed by their original possessors. The Herald Dethick, in 1546, confirmed to Shakespeare, as his coat armour—Or, on a bend sa., a spear of the first. Shelley bore, Sa. a fesse engr. betw. three whelk shells or. In fact, it would be no easy matter to find an ancient coat of arms or badge not allusive to the name, the honour, or estate of the possessor. Clifford says to the Earl of Warwick, in the second part of Henry 6th :—

The Surname "Bacon."

The Surname "Shakespeare."

Shakespeare's application of of Badges as Surnames.

" Might I but know thee by thy household badge"

shows that the name was emblematical of the arms. So much importance was anciently set upon armorial devices that when Henry of Bolingbroke had deprived Richard II. of his crown, he disgraced the Dukes of Albemarle, Holland of Kent, and Earl of Surrey; John Holland, Duke of Exeter, and several others: they were one and all deprived of their armorial bearings and badges of cognizance.

H

CHAPTER IV.

In accounting for the multitude of Buggs and Buggeys, and other branches of these families under other variations of the names, (about 250 families,) I find it necessary to return to a very early period.

The Barons de Roos. Everard de Roos, son of Peter de Roos, Lord of the Manor of Roos, married Rose, his kinswoman, daughter and heir of William Trusbut, in the reign of Henry I. (A.D. 1133.) His grandson, Robert de Roos, appears to have been one of the most turbulent barons of John's reign. As early as the year 1196, the 8th of Richard, he was committed to the custody of Hugh de Chaumont, who "was charged to keep him safe as his own life." He was one of the celebrated 25 barons appointed to enforce the observance of Magna Charta. De Roos married Isabel, daughter of William the Lion, King of Scotland. He died in the year 1226, and was buried in his proper habit of a Knight Templar, in the church of the New Temple, London. From the effigy there of him, on his left arm he bears a heater shaped shield, charged with three water *bougets*, which armorials his grandfather assumed on his marriage with Rose Trusbut. His armorial ensigns are also sculptured upon his shield, and are depicted on the wall of the north aisle They introduce the name into Scotland. of Westminster Abbey. This baron established several of his family in Scotland, whence the name Roos, or Ross, originated. Their armorials are the same, but differenced in tinctures and slightly in marshalling. Mr. Lower, in his Patronymica Britannica, p. 294, says that the Roses of Nairnshire settled there from *temp.* Alexander III. (1249-1285,) origi-

nally wrote themselves De Roos. In 1281, Robert de
Roos, son and heir of the last William, married Isabel,
daughter and heir of William de Albini, lord of Bel-
voir Castle, and whose great-grandfather William, in
the year 1198, married Agatha Trusbut. The original
bearings of the first De Roos were the same as those
of William Fitz-William, son of Ulfr, Jarl of Deira,
under the rule of King Canute. Barry of six ar.
and az. three chaplets of roses.*

In the 5th Henry VI., Thomas, Lord Roos, was
retained in the retinue of John, Duke of Bedford,
with two knights, thirty-seven men-at-arms, and a
hundred and twenty archers, many of whom were
raised on the Roos estates in Bedford, which came
into that family A.D. 1244. And if Mr. Buggey, of
Bedford, can refer to any old official county documents relating to the lordship of Chalveston, in Beds.,

* The name Rose is derived by De Theis, from the Celtic *Origin of*
rhudd, signifying red, whence, he thinks, have originated the synoni- *the names*
mous names *rhos* in Armorican, and *rosha* in Sclavonian, and *roos* in *Rose and*
British. Roses were employed by the Roman emperors as a means *Roos.*
of conferring honours upon their most famous generals, whom they
allowed to add a Rose to the ornaments of the shield (in fact, an
armorial augmentation), a custom which continued long after the
Roman empire had ceased to exist, and the vestiges of which may yet
be traced to the time of Cnut's reign in England. It was a favourite
symbol with the greatest of his few favoured generals, and none
were more so than Ulfr the son of Thorold, sheriff of Lincolnshire
and the grandson of the great Thorold, the first Danish sheriff of
that county, who was also father of the justly celebrated and
benevolent Lady Godiva, Countess of Mercia. This device of Roses
gave the name Roos to a grandson of this Ulfr. Geoffry Fitz
Maldred (of Raby) a descendant of Ulfr's, assumed his wife's surname, Neville, but retained his own arms; hence the origin of the
rose as a badge in the Neville family, and the Barons de Rhos or
Roos, and it is to this day borne entire as a quartering in the
escutcheon of the Duke of Norfolk and the Earl of Carlisle, the
descendants of the grandson Filius William of Ulfr, whose home
was the site of Castle Howard, and whose grand-uncle Liulf,
brother of Ulfr, owned Greystock.

he will find the name of Buggey given ; for it is an invariable rule wherever we find a De Roos, or Ross, lord of a manor, we find tenants named Boog, Bugg, and Boogey, or some of the same names varied in orthography, and called such from the badge which they wore. I hold that this derivation of the name is not only more plausible, but more feasible, than that the same should be derived from Roger de Buci, or Bugey, whose two brothers, Warin and Richard, appear to have had no connection with any other county than that of Lancaster.

The Norman family of de Bugey. Their descendants the Houghtons, of Houghton Tower. In the reign of Rufus, the Manor of Hoghton was given by Warin Buci, with a daughter in frank marriage to Hamo Pincerna, after whose death his wife gave it to their second son, " Ricardus filius Hamonis Pincerna" Butler. The son of Richard Fitz Hamo was Adam, who, in the reign of Henry II., styled himself Adam de Hocton, or Adam Dominus de Hocton.

The Ancient Halls of the Buceys or Bugies. It is somewhat remarkable that King James I., in his journey to the north in 1617, made two stoppages in South Lancashire, and in both instances in the ancient halls of the Bucies—first at Bewsey Hall, in Bewsey Manor, Warrington ; and then at Houghton Tower. Both mansions must have been of very considerable extent, seeing that the King and his entire retinue were provided with accommodation therein.

Robert de Buci, or Busli, is called Bussel, in Testa de Nevill, and mentioned as holding lands in Langton, Leyland, and Eccleston. His descendant is named Hugo Bussel, in the Calendar of the Charter Rolls.

Families descended from the Bugeys, in Lancashire and elsewhere. The Banysters of Newton, Penwortham, and Darwen, were related to the Bucies, and bore their armorials variously differenced ; as also their descendants, the Pemberton's of Pemberton, who bore three water-*buckets*, not *bougets*. The Bushell family, of Myerscough, in Lancashire, are the lineal descendants of the Bucies ; their armorials are Gu. on a chev. erm. three water bougets.

INDEX.

PRINTED BY JOHN HEYWOOD, 143, DEANSGATE, MANCHESTER.

www.ingramcontent.com/pod-product-compliance
Lightning Source LLC
Chambersburg PA
CBHW030019030726
47499CB00008B/3054